Weighing the Elephant

Story by Ting-xing Ye

Art by Suzane Langlois

Annick Press • Toronto • New York

Long ago, in the green mountains of China, the village called Beyond the Clouds was ruled by a cruel and clever emperor. But the mountains were high, and the Emperor was far away. The warm climate and fertile soil, and especially the help of a neighbouring elephant family, provided the hard-working farmers with a prosperous and peaceful life. The villagers took great care of the friendly elephants, particularly the baby, Huan-huan.

Huan-huan's mother and father were super-giants; at least, that was what their young keeper, Hei-dou, proudly claimed. Their bulky bodies were taller than any house in the village and thicker than the wall of the Emperor's palace. And their ears were so broad that only the biggest banana leaves could match them.

As for baby Huan-huan, since the day he was born it seemed that every breath of air he took lifted him up an inch and each passing breeze added to his weight.

Every day Hei-dou rose at daybreak and headed out to fetch the elephants. Mother took the lead, closely followed by Hei-dou and Huan-huan, and Father ambled along behind. Their trunks hung casually, their ears flapped to drive away the flies and their flat feet rustled softly on the path to the village.

During the day, while his elephant parents were busy hauling logs, pulling carts, toting bags of grain and barrels of water, or carrying the villagers up on their backs, Huan-huan stayed with Hei-dou and the other schoolchildren. Using his supple trunk, he retrieved balls and shuttlecocks that had landed on the roof and rescued kites and paper birds caught in the trees.

Best of all, when school was out he stood up on his hind feet, fanned his ears and danced, with all the children singing and swirling around him.

At dusk, Huan-huan joined his parents at the shore, where they drank from the lake, ate succulent green grass and gave each other a shower or powdered themselves with sand. Hei-dou always waited and then took them home.

Word of Huan-huan's friendliness and resourcefulness travelled fast and far, and soon reached the palace. Although there were over fifty of the best elephants to carry the Imperial Family and entertain their guests, the Emperor was not satisfied.

"I am the Emperor and I should have the best of everything!" he roared. And he sent his soldiers to bring Huan-huan to him.

"He's only a baby," Hei-dou pleaded with the Emperor's soldiers.

"It's the Emperor's order," growled the captain of the guards, thumping his spear against his shield.

Hei-dou turned to the villagers. "Can't we do something?" he cried. But the farmers stood silently with heads bowed as Huan-huan was taken away.

The angry trumpeting of Huan-huan's mother and father filled the evening sky.

Inside the palace, the young Prince pointed his sword at Huan-huan and screamed, "Show me all your tricks!"

"Water all my flowers," shouted the little Princess, perched on a soldier's shoulders and waving her tiny fists. "Do what I say!"

The Empress's long face was like a twisted rope. "Make the Prince laugh and bring a smile to the Princess," she commanded.

"Obey them or you will be punished," ordered the Emperor, his fat body quaking with every word.

Where are my parents? Huan-huan wondered. Where are Hei-dou and the other children? Sad and confused, he lowered himself to the ground, let out a long and heavy sigh, and closed his eyes.

Every day, the Prince shouted himself hoarse, the Princess could hardly keep her eyes dry, the Empress stamped her feet sore with fury and the Emperor's teeth ground so loudly that they could be heard outside the palace wall. But frightened Huan-huan remained frozen to the spot.

One day, Hei-dou led Huan-huan's parents to the palace to beg for their baby's return, only to be chased away by the soldiers long before they approached the gate.

Finally, the angry Emperor decreed an imperial punishment for Huan-huan's disobedience: he was to be heavily chained and sent far, far away, never to see his parents again.

"If the Emperor doesn't want him, why not give him back to the village?" the farmers pleaded with the messenger. "Please ask the Emperor if we can keep him!"

Pulling Huan-huan along behind him with a rope, the messenger returned with a new edict from the palace: "The baby elephant will be taken away in two days unless someone can tell me, the Emperor, how heavy he is."

Hei-dou and the villagers fell silent, for they knew it was a trick. Besides his cruelty and ferociousness, the Emperor was notorious for absurd riddles that often had no solutions.

He had once ordered a fisherman to tell him the number of scales on a live fish. The poor man failed, and the Emperor confiscated his day's catch. The Emperor had also commanded a farmer to count the hairs on his ox. The farmer had no answer, so the ox was slaughtered to feed the Emperor's guests.

A dark cloud shadowed the village. Two days was not much time. Where to start? How to begin?

"Send for the scholars!" someone suggested.

"Bring all the scales to the village square!" another advised.

Quickly the butchers collected their pole-scales, long and short, thin and thick. The shopkeepers brought their counter-scales, round and square, big and small. The farmers pushed the heavy warehouse scales, as tall as Hei-dou's reach and wide as his embrace, into the crowd.

Scholar East broke the silence first, his thin goat-beard moving up and down when he spoke. "Weigh each leg at a time, then add the four numbers."

"Then how can we weigh the elephant?" Hei-dou asked. "How can we save Huan-huan from being sent away?"

"Don't panic," Scholar North said calmly, pointing to the large warehouse scales sitting on the ground. "Place one of his feet on each scale at the same time. *Then* add the four numbers."

"No, no, no, my dear fellow. You forgot his heavy head, long trunk, two fan-like ears and new tusks," sneered Scholar South.

"And his round chubby belly!" Scholar West added.

"What a shame!" Scholar North scolded in a dry voice, shaking his head. "Such silly ideas will never work."

Hei-dou helped the farmers arrange the scales. Once, twice, ten times and twenty, until Hei-dou lost count, poor Huan-huan tried to do as the shouting villagers urged— until suddenly a loud cheer went up as the baby elephant finally managed to balance himself on the scales. But almost immediately a sharp clang rang out as the iron counter-weights sprang into the air and thumped to the ground. Terrified, Huan-huan jumped back off the scales.

Evening came. Sadly Hei-dou said goodbye to
Huan-huan and his parents and walked down to the lake,
hoping that tomorrow would never come. How he wished he could
run off with Huan-huan. But where could they go? Everywhere they
set foot was the Emperor's land. Through tears, he watched the
moon push through the thick clouds and dance above the water,
casting silver light on his father's fishing boat.

Then a thought surged into his mind. He dashed back home and
waited impatiently for dawn to arrive.

Before sunrise Hei-dou was ready. As he and the plodding elephants walked into the village, people gathered around.

"I know how to weigh Huan-huan," Hei-dou announced.

"How could you succeed where our scholars have failed?" one farmer scoffed.

Another smirked, "You are not even old enough to handle the smallest scale!"

Even his own parents looked doubtful.

"Please," Hei-dou pleaded. "Let me try."

From the distance came the ominous sound of galloping horses.

Hei-dou winked at Huan-huan and whispered into his ear. He then guided the baby elephant to the shore and stopped before his father's boat. At Hei-dou's suggestion, eight strong farmers waded into the lake to hold the boat steady. Gingerly Huan-huan followed Hei-dou along the plank and into the centre of the boat, which quickly settled deep into the water. Hei-dou slipped into the lake and, taking a piece of charcoal from his pocket, carefully drew a solid black line at the water level along the side of the boat.

As soon as he and Huan-huan were back on shore, Hei-dou said loudly, trying to contain his excitement, "Please, everybody, help to carry rice bags into the boat until..."

His father stopped him. "— until the black mark is level with the water again, and..."

"— and," said his mother, "weigh the bags, one at a time, then..."

"— Then add up all the numbers!" another exclaimed.

Everyone chimed in, "The total will be the weight of Huan-huan!"

When the soldiers returned to the palace without Huan-huan and reported what they had seen in the village, the Emperor was speechless.

Red-faced and fuming, he threw the soldiers out and sank into his chair like a deflated balloon. He remained there for the rest of the day, the rest of the week, and the rest of the month. And he never posed another tricky riddle.

Laughter returned to the village, and there were smiles on every face. In the schoolyard, Huan-huan rose up on his hind feet and, encircled by the singing children, began to dance. But that day, it seemed he danced only for Hei-dou.

Author's note:

The name Hei-dou (pronounced *Hay-dough*) means "black bean".
Huan-huan's name (pronounced H*wan* as in S*wan*) means "cheerful".

For Bill
—T.Y.

To Samuel, Jean-Remi, David and Alexis
—S.L.

We acknowledge the support of the Canada Council for the Arts
for our publishing program. We also thank the Ontario Arts Council.

Cataloguing in Publication Data

Ye, Ting-xing, 1952-
Weighing the elephant

ISBN 1-55037-527-X (bound)   ISBN 1-55037-526-1 (pbk.)

I. Langlois, Suzane. II. Title.

PS8597.E16W44 1998   jC813'.54   C98-930309-8
PZ7.Y4We 1998

The art in this book was rendered in watercolours.
The text was typeset in Baskerville.

Distributed in Canada by:
Firefly Books Ltd.
3680 Victoria Park Avenue
Willowdale, ON
M2H 3K1

Published in the U.S.A. by
Annick Press (U.S.) Ltd.
Distributed in the U.S.A. by:
Firefly Books (U.S.) Inc.
P.O. Box 1338, Ellicott Station
Buffalo, NY 14205

Printed and bound in Canada by
Friesens, Altona, Manitoba.